PIG

and the
Talking Poo

Barbara Catchpole

Illustrated by metaphrog

RANSOM

Say 'Hello'

to Peter Ian Green

- 'PIG' for short.

There are six PIG books so far. It's best to read them in this order:

1. **PIG** and the **Talking Poo**
2. **PIG** and the **Fancy Pants**
3. **PIG** and the **Long Fart**
4. **PIG** plays **Cupid**
5. **PIG** gets the **Black Death** (nearly)
6. **PIG** Saves the **Day**

PIG and the Talking Poo
by Barbara Catchpole
Illustrated by metaphrog

Published by Ransom Publishing Ltd.
Unit 7, Brocklands Farm, West Meon, Hampshire
GU32 1JN, UK
www.ransom.co.uk

ISBN   978 184167 520 6
First published in 2012
Reprinted 2013, 2014, 2015

Copyright © 2012 Ransom Publishing Ltd.
Illustrations copyright © 2012 metaphrog

A CIP catalogue record of this book is available from the British Library.

Me

Hi! As this story about the Poo is the first story I have to tell you, I am going to tell you about my family. Then you can tell me about your family and we can be mates.

My name is Pig.

Me

Really it's Peter Ian Green, but all my friends and family call me Pig. Even the teachers call me Pig. A bit rude, I think, but you can't tell them, can you?

I am 12 and I am small for my age. I have sticky-out ears and bright red hair, which is also sticky-up.

Here is a photo of me on holiday dressed as a pirate. It was one of those competitions – you know the kind. I didn't win anything and I kept bumping into things because of the patch. It was a swizz.

Us

I live with my mum. I am small for my age but my mum is huge for hers. Here is a picture of my mum's head. We couldn't get the rest of her in the space.

She is a single mum but she looks more like a double mum or even a treble mum. Mum has the loudest laugh in the world — it comes right from deep down in her belly. When she is angry, though — watch out! Run away!

When I was nine I put a piece of toast down the toilet because I didn't want it. She told me

she had fished it out and she made me eat it!
Toilet toast. I can't remember what it tasted
like, but I bet it was yuk.

My big sister, Suki, lives with us but Mum says
she should

> 'Go and get her own flat and eat her own
> food. The cheek she's got at her age! Hope
> she's going to look after me when I'm old!
> Not holding my breath ...'

Suki wears huge hoop earrings and huge high
heels. She jangles
and clicks when
she walks. She has
a loud laugh, too.

My Gran says she has a laugh

'like a plane going through the sound barrier,'

and

'she can get Radio One on them earrings'.

I also have a baby brother who is pink, loud, wet and smelly – and doesn't know that you sleep when it's dark.

There's not a lot to say about him except it was

quieter before we had him. And less smelly.

Oh. And he has a special name. One day I'll tell you what it is. (I think that's called suspense.)

Then there's Gran, who is

'always round our house drinking our tea.'

(Mum said that.)

She's Dad's mum, not Mum's mum. Her teeth

have fallen out and she smells a bit funny – like floor polish. She smells like the hall floor when you come back after a holiday. But she's not as shiny.

Dad

Where is Dad? At the moment nobody knows, but my mum says

> 'He'd better not show his face round here in a hurry.'

I was a bit upset when he stopped seeing me at weekends, but I'm OK now. I don't think about him at all.

He was the one who bought the Poo. It's really

great. It's a huge brown plastic dog poo. Not one of those long ones like a cigar that's gone dry. No, it's a curly brown wet-looking poo, with a little black plastic fly on it.

My talking poo.

It looks like one of those, when you tread on it, it gets in the grooves of your trainers and you have to wash them if you don't want it to come off on the carpet and get your mum mad.

That kind of poo really smells, doesn't it? You know the sort of poo – you have to get it out of all the grooves with a safety pin, if you can find one. Last time I saw Dad, I was eleven then, he took me to McDonalds and he bought me the Poo. In a joke shop, not in McDonalds.

I lost the Poo for a long time, but last week I found it in Mum's dressing table (I wonder how it got there?).

It's been talking to me ever since.

Hello Pig!

13

Yesterday the Poo told me I should take it into school and put it on the teacher's chair. So that's what I decided to do.

Then they will sit on me. Ha ha!

I should tell you three things:

One

I do know the Poo is not really talking to me. I'm not bonkers or anything.

Two

I was looking for a safety pin.

Three

I just love Jack Bauer in 24, so this book is about 24 hours in my life.

(P.S. in brackets: if you don't know who Jack Bauer is, look it up. On the Internet or something. You might be able to do it in your ICT lesson, before your teacher notices, if you're quick. I talk about Jack Bauer a lot. That's how awesome he is.)

Anyway my family is cool. Best family ever.

We all have red hair too, except Gran who says

'my red has washed off'.

Some of her hair has washed off too.

Oh eight hundred hours

I edged my way downstairs
with my back to the wall
and the Poo in one hand.

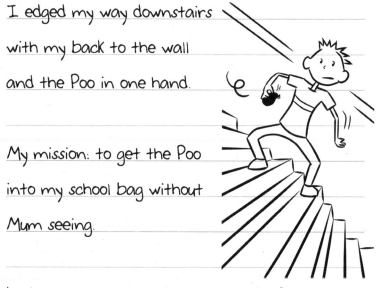

My mission: to get the Poo
into my school bag without
Mum seeing.

Luckily our hamster, Harry, named after

Houdini (look him up, too) thinks he is a prisoner of war. He thinks it is his duty to escape.

Harry had got out again and was stuck in the hoover pipe, so Mum was a bit busy.

I walked to school with my best friend, Raj. He is a Sikh and has long hair tied up in a cloth on his head.

He is going to grow a beard when he grows up. He keeps looking at his chin in the boys' loo in between lessons, as if he might have grown a beard in Maths.

I told him about my Poo plan. He said what he always says to me:

> 'Oh, Pig, this will end in trouble, I can see it. I can see it, Pig.'

Raj's mum says I am a Bad Influence on Raj.

I hope I am. He worries too much. He needs some fun in his life.

Oh nine hundred hours

I've forgotten what assembly was about because I could see that the girl in front of me had nits and they were skiing down her pony tail. So I didn't listen.

I never listen in assembly. Except the one when

they had snakes. That one was cool.

So now I am not going to sit next to any girl with long hair until Christmas, as they will now all have nits. Nits are like farts – nobody can see them, but they spread out quickly.

I didn't use the Poo in Maths because the Maths teacher was away again and the headteacher took us. I don't know what she can do to me, but it is her school so there must be something bad she can do.

I'm scared of her!

Ten hundred hours

PE. Football. Mud. Brilliant.

We won and I was in goal. Nine – six.

Jack Meaney had a nosebleed.

Eleven hundred

We had double Science. Now I didn't use the

Poo in Science for two reasons.

Reason 1

We had a lesson where we had to solve a crime from the evidence. I was Gil Grissom off CSI and Raj was that cool black guy who has a gambling problem. We really got into it.

(P.S. in brackets again: don't tell me you don't know who Gil Grissom is. There must be about ten zillion CSI episodes!)

Reason 2

I forgot.

Twelve hundred hours

It was Friday so it was chips.

It took a long time to get to the front, because

on chips day everyone has school dinner. When

it is salad day, you can get fed in half the time.

The chip queue went all the way round the hall

and there were fights over big kids pushing in.

Raj and I pushed in as much as we could get

away with in front of the girls. Some of the

girls are very scary. You push in front of them

and you might end up eating lunch in hospital (through a straw).

The dinner lady with the red hair gave me a huge pile of chips. I couldn't see over it!

She said:

'We've got to stick together, Carrot-top!'

By the time it came to sitting down there were only two places left in our bit – on the end of a bench and next to Kelsey Davis. We raced but I

lost and had to sit next to Kelsey.

I hate her. I know it is wrong, but I do.

I really, really, really hate her. She cries all the

time – just cries – for no reason.

Once in lower school she stole Hettie

Greenbum's mobile phone. (She wasn't really

called Hettie Greenbum – her name was

Greenburn, but – well, you know ...)

So Miss was, like:

>'How can we tell who has stolen it?'

So I go:

>'Phone the number.'

So there it was in Kelsey's bag. Crazy Frog

playing from her horrid pink bag. So I say:

>'There's your thief!'

Then Kelsey started crying and saying she only picked it up by MISTAKE (very likely, I don't think).

Wah, wah, wah, wah: like a police car. I had to say I was sorry!

She still cries whenever she sees me – and that was in lower school. It was more than a YEAR ago! I hate her and the stupid, pink flower in her stupid, long nitty hair.

As I ate my chips I got to thinking. How much would she cry if she found a poo in her food? Should be worth seeing, I thought.

I shouted:

'Look over there!'

And she did. She looked over there.

I put the Poo between her chips and her peas.

When she saw it, she went very still. Then she went a green colour. Then she started to make a little sobbing noise. Then she really got going and screamed. Her face went red, then purple.

Spit flew out of her mouth. It was awesome.

Teachers came running from all over the hall.

She carried on forever, until one of the dinner

ladies said she was

'historical' and threw a

glass of water over her.

Kelsey shut up then – just

sat there dripping.

I finished my last chip and
went to get the Poo back,
but the plate was gone.

The Poo had disappeared!

Thirteen hundred hours

At first I thought it was lost forever. I didn't
cry (of course), but I was pretty choked. My
dad had bought me that poo!

Raj is much cleverer than I am, though. (I
don't mind, it's just a fact.) He said:

    'Don't sweat it, Pig! It'll be in the Big Bins.'

The Big Bins are at the back of the kitchens. They are huge. They are so big that there is a little ladder on the outside for the dinner ladies to climb up and put the mucky food that is left into them from the small kitchen bins.

Every Friday afternoon special giant dustmen come and fix the Big Bins onto the big

council lorry that grinds everything up in a big round knife thing and takes it to the dump.

I had to rescue the Poo!

We got Wayne Baggott to tell the Humanities teacher that I had been sick and Raj was taking me to the nurse. Then we walked all round the school to the Big Bins.

(I had to say I would let Wayne score a goal next PE lesson – but I won't. He's rubbish at football.)

The bins were huge. Only one had its lid open and I thought that must be the one.

Raj was very unhappy to be skipping lessons (again) and I had to offer him half my chips next Friday to make him keep look-out.

I climbed up and looked into the mess of brown goo, cold chips, baked beans and more brown goo. Suddenly, amongst all the brown I could see it. It had nearly sunk. The Poo! MY Poo!

The only problem was: the bin was not very full and it was below where I could reach. Raj would have to climb up and hold my legs as I reached down.

He was more happy to help than I thought he would be. He told me afterwards it was because he was sure he saw a rat watching him down on the ground. He said it was bigger than a football and was looking at him and licking its lips!

Anyway, Raj held me by my waist and I leaned down into the Big Bin. It was gross in there.

The smell was terrible, like rotting brussel sprouts
and baby nappies. I could just about get it, my
Poo. My fingers felt it. I couldn't get a grip.

Then I had it - but I dropped it.

Suddenly, it all happened at once. My trousers
slipped off, Raj grabbed at me and somehow we
both fell deep into the brown mess in the

bottom of the bin.

At first I felt panic. I got a mouthful of muck and thought I would drown. The smell made me cry. Well, not CRY. You know, it just got in my eyes and made them water. A bit.

Raj pulled me up and I pulled my trousers up. They had cold food in them.

We found we could both stand, up to our waists in cold school dinners. Good job it wasn't a lot deeper. That really would have been gross.

Raj had baked beans stuck up his nose and a cabbage leaf on his head. I could feel the goo seeping into my shoes. I looked down and I really thought it was moving. It was like that bit in Star Wars, except the walls didn't start closing in.

Raj said

    'What are we going to do? Look at us! Help!

    Help!'

Raj shouted 'Help' - but the sound just went round and round the bin. He said:

'We could stay in here all night. They will never find us.'

I said:

'No, we will not stay in here all night.'

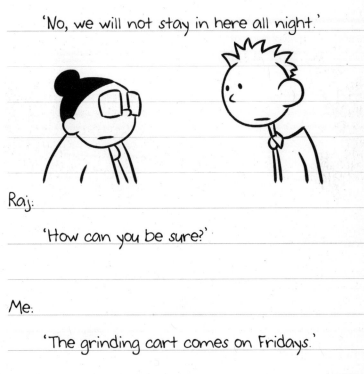

Raj:

'How can you be sure?'

Me:

'The grinding cart comes on Fridays.'

Fourteen hundred hours

We heard the grinding cart coming. Then there was silence, apart from the noise of Raj muttering something in Punjabi.

'I'm sorry I got you into this, Raj.'

'You are a bad influence.'

'Yes, I am.'

'We are going to die!'

'Yes, we are!'

I thought maybe I should say something nice to Raj. Should I hug him or something? He was going to give his life for the Talking Poo!

No, there was no need to go all girly.

　'Thanks, Raj!'

　'It's OK.'

We could hear banging on the outside of the bin. I nearly wet myself.

But we didn't die. Something much worse happened. Our mothers found us.

My mother's face looked over the top of the

bin.

She said:

'Thank God you're safe, Pig. I am going to

kill you!'

I grabbed the Poo and shoved it in my pocket

next to the cold baked beans.

Then a dustman pulled us both out and we stood cold and filthy, like swamp monsters, while our mothers shouted at us.

Mrs Kaur told my mother I was a bad influence and my mother agreed.

But then my mother said:

'Your Raj should stand up for himself.'

I thought they might have a fight but no, Mrs Kaur agreed.

'You are right. He is too weak. He is like his father.'

They both nodded their heads up and down sadly while we watched them, covered in bean goo.

The school had phoned my mum and Mrs Kaur to say we were missing. My mum had picked up

Mrs Kaur and they had come looking for us. She had been sure we were hiding round the back of the school. Then she'd heard us in the bin.

The headteacher came out to the car park just to shout at us.

Then we had to take off our clothes, down to our pants, in the car park and sit on bin bags in the car.

We were standing there in our pants when the girls' hockey team went past. They all whistled and called out rude stuff.

Fifteen hundred hours

Mum was very angry. She shouted at me a lot.

I told her shouting wouldn't change me and she said no, but it made her feel better, so she didn't care.

She made me wash all
my clothes by hand.
The cold food had to be
pushed down the plug
hole with my fingers.

Then she sent me to bed. At fifteen hundred
hours! That never happened to Jack Bauer.

Nobody crosses Jack Bauer. I bet his mum
couldn't have made him stay in his bedroom
without a telly.

I had to read a book (a book!) and all I got for
my tea was cold toast. Really cold toast. I
reckon she'd put it in the fridge before she gave
it to me.

Oh seven hundred hours
Saturday morning

Mum works at Tesco's at oh eight hundred hours on Saturdays, but she got me out of bed at oh seven hundred hours just to get me to iron my school clothes. She made me thank her for taking the trouble.

I burned my finger and Mum said I needed to do a lot more ironing so I could get better at it.

We sat down at the kitchen table and she said:

'Now tell me what mad, nutty, stupid,

reason you had for falling into a giant bin.'

I told her about the Poo and how it talked to

me.

She said:

'P-I-I-I-I-G!'

She spoke quietly, but I could see she was angry.

I thought about it. Yes, I was telling fibs.
Sometimes I can't really tell.

I said:

'I'm sorry. I know he doesn't really talk to
me. But I really like him.'

'But I don't understand, Pig. Why did you
have to go get it? Why not just buy another
one, if you must have that disgusting thing?'

'Because Dad bought him for me.'

Then she came round and put her arm round me and hugged me. I think she was crying a bit.

'And it reminds me of Dad.'

Mum said:

'I can see why, Pig. It reminds me of Dad too. Very much!'

She laughed her big laugh and I started laughing too, and we just fell about laughing together.

I didn't cry, but my eyes watered a bit.

The next **PIG** book is

PIG
and the
Fancy Pants

About the author

Barbara Catchpole was a teacher for thirty years and enjoyed every minute. She has three sons of her own who were always perfectly behaved and never gave her a second of worry.

Barbara also tells lies.